THE CHILDREN'S CLASSICS Collection

Dados Internacionais de Catalogação na Publicação (CIP) de acordo com ISBD

K57t Kipling, Rudyard.
The jungle book / Rudyard Kipling. - Jandira, SP : W. Books, 2025.
120 p. : 12,80cm x 19,80cm. - (Classics).

ISBN: 978-65-5294-124-4

1. Literatura inglesa. 2. Séries. 3. Clássicos. 4. Filmes. 5. Aventura. I. Título.
II. Série.

2025-2476 CDD 820
CDU 821.111-3

Elaborada por Lucio Feitosa - CRB-8/8803
Índice para catálogo sistemático:
1. Literatura inglesa 820
2. Literatura inglesa 821.111-3

Text based on the original story by Rudyard Kipling,
adapted by Gemma Barder
Illustrations by Archina Laezza

1st edition in 2025
www.cirandacultural.com.br

THE JUNGLE BOOK

Rudyard Kipling

W. Books

Mowgli

A man cub

Akela

Leader of the wolf pack

Mother and Father Wolf

Mowgli's wolf parents

Grey

Mowgli's wolf brother

Messua

A woman in the man village

Shere Khan

A fearsome tiger

Kaa

A greedy python

Bandar

A giant monkey

Bagheera

A wise panther

Baloo

A friendly bear

Chapter One

A chorus of croaks and craws could be heard all around the Indian jungle. It was home to animals big and small. Many flew through the trees, others slithered through the swamp and some hid in the shadows to avoid being seen or heard.

Somewhere, deep in the twisted depths, a young boy stumbled along the undergrowth. The way he walked on two legs and his

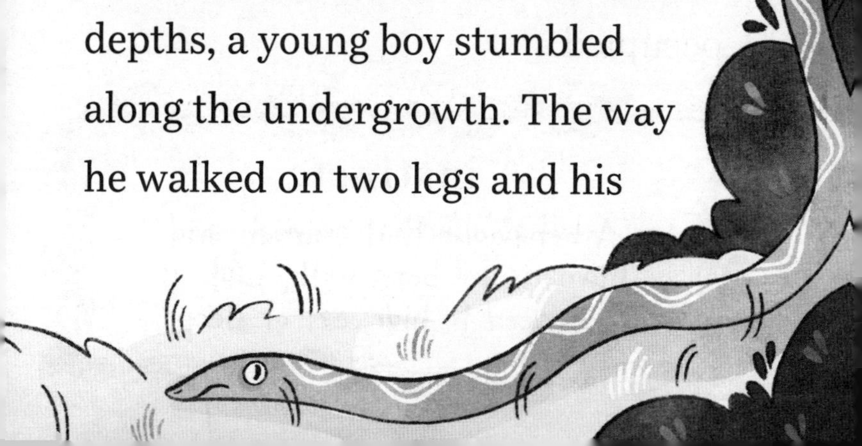

lack of fur, or scales, had caught the attention of a pair of piercing yellow eyes. Those eyes were watching the boy's every move. Watching, and waiting.

The young boy came to the mouth of a small cave. By instinct, he crawled inside and sat hugging his knees. He could not remember the last time he saw his mother and father and his stomach growled with hunger. He was too exhausted to notice that the cave was already occupied.

instinct

A behaviour that animals and humans are born with, such as the need to hide, eat or sleep.

‘What kind of creature is that?’ said Mother Wolf, staring at the boy. Her cubs slept silently in a huddle at her feet.

‘I think it is a man cub,’ said Father Wolf, stepping closer to the peculiar creature.

'Be careful!' said Mother Wolf. 'You know how humans treat animals.'

Father Wolf took another step closer to examine the boy. 'Not this one, he's barely old enough to walk.'

Mother Wolf padded out of the shadows to sniff the little boy. He did not flinch or try to run away when he saw their sharp teeth and long claws. He looked at them in wonder. Then, he reached out to Mother

Wolf's grey mane and stroked it.

'The poor thing, out here all alone,' said Mother Wolf, licking the top of the boy's head and making him giggle.

Suddenly, Father Wolf began to growl. He lowered himself to the ground and stared out into the inky darkness beyond the cave entrance.

'What's the matter?' asked Mother Wolf.

'I think your mate might be warning you of *my* arrival,' said

Shere Khan, slinking lazily out of the jungle. 'The man cub is mine. You will kindly hand him over.'

Mother Wolf stepped out of the cave to join Father Wolf. She glanced back into the darkness where the innocent man cub sat and where her cubs were safe and sleeping.

mate

One of a pair of animals that live or have a family together.

'Shere Khan,' said Mother Wolf sternly, positioning herself in front of the cave's entrance. 'You are mistaken. This man cub is mine. He is part of our pack.'

Shere Khan laughed. 'Yours?' he said. 'Well, if that is true then he must have been accepted by the *whole* of the wolf pack, is that right? Does Akela know of his existence?'

Mother and Father Wolf looked at each other. The tiger was right. Any new member of the wolf pack had to be accepted by the pack leader, Akela. 'We will present him at the council of wolves tomorrow night at Council Rock,' said Father Wolf.

'Then he will have the protection of all of us.'

Shere Khan smiled, wickedly. '*If* he is accepted,' he said. 'If not, the boy is mine.'

Chapter Two

‘We’ll call the man cub Mowgli,’ said Mother Wolf. ‘And we will raise him as our own.’

Father Wolf stared at the small, furless creature. ‘But will the pack accept him? He’s not a wolf, my dear, he’s a man,’ he said. ‘And we all know what men do when they grow up. They kill animals like us.’

‘Then he will be different,’ said

Mother Wolf. 'And we can't hand him over to Shere Khan. You know what he will do to him. Shere Khan hates humans. We would be sending the poor thing to certain death.'

The following evening, Akela, the alpha and leader of the wolf pack, sat high on Council Rock, a sharp tilting piece of land that overlooked the jungle.

Beneath him, his pack of wolves assembled. News of the man cub had spread across the jungle. More than just the wolves had turned up to witness the council meeting. Snakes, bears, panthers and even an old elephant stood nearby to listen in.

The shuffling of hooves and paws hushed as the drum of Shere Khan's giant paws padded along the jungle floor. The crowd separated as the tiger prowled through.

'You wish for this man cub to become part of our pack?' Akela asked Father Wolf, loud enough for the gathered animals to hear.

'Yes, Akela,' replied Father Wolf, nudging Mowgli forward. 'We ask that he has the same protection as the rest of our litter of cubs.'

Akela looked over at the small boy. His dark hair flopped over his eyes and he brushed it out of his face before staring back up at the old wolf. 'He certainly doesn't seem to be afraid of us,' said Akela.

'That is precisely why he should be handed over to me,' said Shere Khan, who stood front and centre of the bustling crowd of animals. 'This boy will grow into a *man* and hunt the innocent animals of the jungle just as every other human has done before him. If he is unafraid now, what will he be like when he is fully grown? It is better that he is killed now.'

'We won't let that happen,' growled Father Wolf, baring his teeth at Shere Khan in warning.

'Settle down,' said Akela. 'To be accepted by the wolf pack, the man cub must be spoken for by two members who are not his mother and father. These two animals will help to raise him if he is to stay in the pack and teach him the laws of the jungle.'

The crowd of animals hushed. There was no answer and Mother Wolf began to fear the worst. How could she expect two animals to help her and Father Wolf look after a man cub?

The long silence was finally broken by a deep voice coming from a tree above Council Rock. ‘Perhaps I can help,’ purred Bagheera the panther. His sleek black shadow dropped from the tree branch onto the rock where Akela stood. He walked past Shere Khan without meeting his eye. ‘I have watched the man village for many years, I believe I know a little about how men think, and

I can teach the man cub some skills he might need as he grows.'

'Me too!' said a great, brown bear, stumbling out of the jungle towards the group. 'I can help the little scrap defend himself.'

Mother Wolf's eyes darted toward the bear in surprise.

Bagheera rolled his eyes. 'Baloo, I hardly think–'

'It is decided!' Akela said, loud

enough to stop Bagheera from talking. 'The man cub named Mowgli has the protection of the pack!'

Mother Wolf let out a sigh of relief.

Shere Khan gave off a low growl in frustration. 'Do not make the mistake of thinking this is the end, Akela,' he said. 'It is only a matter of time before the man cub is mine. I'm very good at waiting.'

Before Akela could change his mind, Mother Wolf picked up Mowgli by the cloth he wore around his body and took him back to their cave. From that day on, he would have the pack's protection.

Shere Khan narrowed his eyes as he watched. 'This isn't over,' he growled. 'I will kill Mowgli. Just wait and see.' And with that, Shere Khan disappeared into the thick leaves and left the jungle.

Chapter Three

As Mowgli grew up, Bagheera and Baloo were true to their word. They looked out for the boy and played an active part in his upbringing.

They often spent days with Mowgli, teaching him the laws of the jungle. From every rustle in the grass to each squawk of a bird.

When Mowgli had just turned eleven, Baloo decided it was time to teach him the Master Words.

'Honestly Baloo, do you not think that is *my* job?' asked Bagheera, as he paced around the bear and Mowgli. 'I am in charge of the boy's … intellectual growth.'

Baloo sniffed and scratched his tummy. 'That might be true, Baggy,' he said. 'But I'm teaching the boy how to look after himself and we all know the Master Words will help him do just that.'

The Master Words were a set of words that could be spoken and more importantly *understood* by

intellect

Someone's ability to understand and solve difficult situations or ideas.

any animal in the jungle. From a tiny mosquito, right up to a mighty elephant.

The only trouble was, Mowgli was far more interested in playing with Grey, his wolf brother, than learning. Grey leapt out of the jungle into the clearing, sending Mowgli flying to the ground in shrieks of laughter.

'Grey!' scolded Bagheera, pinning the cub to the ground with one of his big black paws. 'Get back to the den this minute. Mowgli has work to do.'

'But Bagheera!' said Mowgli. 'I don't want to have lessons! I want to play! Baloo? Tell him!'

Baloo sighed. 'Sorry, kid,' he said. 'I agree with Bagheera on this one. You've got to learn the words, they might help you one day.'

As a disappointed Grey padded back to the wolf den, his tail between his legs,

Mowgli grumpily sat on the floor of the clearing.

Baloo and Bagheera slowly began to recite the Master Words, and what each one meant. After an hour, Mowgli could feel his eyelids begin to droop.

The jungle was getting hotter as the day wore on. 'Come now,' said Bagheera. 'One more time.'

Mowgli groaned. 'But I *know* them!' he said. 'Can't we go and cool off at the watering hole?'

Baloo shook his head. 'Not today, kid,' he said. 'How about tomorrow? I'll take you there myself and you can float on my tummy like last time.'

Mowgli kicked the dirt. 'Why do *I* have to have lessons all the time?' he said. 'Grey and the other cubs get to be taught by Mother and Father. It isn't fair.'

Bagheera and Baloo looked at each other. 'Well, because you aren't like the other cubs,' said Bagheera, carefully. 'You are a man cub. You need a bit of extra help in case–'

'I know, I know,' said Mowgli, with a sigh. 'In case Shere Khan comes back to the jungle.' Suddenly, Mowgli jumped up. His hands balled into fists. 'Maybe I *want* him to come back, anyway,' said Mowgli, angrily. 'Then I can fight him and show everyone how brave I am!'

‘Mowgli, Shere Khan is a tiger,’ warned Bagheera. ‘He has killed many humans before and he will spare no thought about killing you, too.’

Mowgli got up. ‘It’s not fair!’ he shouted and shot off into the dark depths of the jungle.

Bagheera went to chase after him, but Baloo placed a steadying paw on his back. ‘Let the little man cool off for a bit,’ he said. ‘He’ll come back when he’s ready.’

Chapter Four

Mowgli ran until his legs grew tired. He knew that he would have to go back to Bagheera and Baloo at some point, but right now he wanted to be on his own. He wasn't angry at them, really. He knew they were only trying to protect him, but sometimes Mowgli wished he could be just like everyone else. He wished that he had fur and ran on four legs like his siblings, or prowled though the jungle like Bagheera, or was as tough and strong as Baloo.

As he leant against the trunk of a tree and sheltered in its cool shade, Mowgli closed his eyes for a moment.

Suddenly, he felt a warm hand on his arm. His eyes shot open in alarm just in time to see that a group of young monkeys had surrounded him. They yanked Mowgli's arm and snatched him up into the trees. They swung him through the air as they flew from branch to branch.

'Hey!' shouted Mowgli. 'Let me go!' But the monkeys just laughed and chattered as they carried him further away. Deeper into the jungle.

Mowgli tried to catch his breath as the trees whirled past his face. He struggled to figure out which way was up and he started to feel dizzy.

Then, Mowgli spotted Rann the kite swooping high above him. He knew the bird to be wise and fair, and was sure she would help him, but Mowgli had never spoken to a bird before.

Mowgli's mind raced. He knew he had to act fast. He had no idea where the monkeys were taking him and soon his opportunity to get home might be lost.

Mowgli called to the bird using the Master Words Baloo and Bagheera had taught him earlier that day. He prayed Rann would understand.

The great bird swept down and watched as she saw the group of monkeys carrying the man cub through the jungle. With a slight nod of her head, Rann flew off.

Baloo scratched the back of his head and stared at the spot where

Mowgli had run into the jungle. 'He should have been back by now,' he said. 'He's never taken off for this long before.'

'If you had let me go after him when I wanted to–' said Bagheera.

'All right, all right,' said Baloo, holding up his paws. 'I know. I feel bad enough as it is. I keep forgetting how little he still is.

I shouldn't have been so tough on him.'

Bagheera sighed. 'Maybe we haven't been tough enough,' he said. 'Mowgli's life here is only going to get harder as he gets older. Shere Khan won't let him grow into a man without a fight.'

Just then, the bear and panther were interrupted by the shriek of a bird from above them. Rann swooped into the clearing and folded her wings as she spoke: 'The man cub,' squawked Rann,

‘He’s been taken by the monkeys.’

Bagheera and Baloo sprang up. ‘Where are they taking him?’ asked Bagheera, jumping on his toes, ready to run.

‘I couldn’t be certain, but I would say they were headed to the ancient ruins,’ replied Rann.

‘Wait just a second,’ said Baloo. ‘How did you know where to find us?’

Rann began to stretch out her wings, ready to take flight again. ‘The man cub told me,’ she said. ‘The boy has a good knowledge of the Master Words. Now go!’

Chapter Five

Mowgli sat in the middle of the ancient ruins. Vines crept over every brick and pillar of the crumbling structure. Monkeys of every shape and size clambered around him, chattering and pulling his hair.

Mowgli tried to shrug them off, scanning the ruins for a way to escape.

At that moment, a large monkey with flowing fur appeared from out of the shadows. It was larger than any monkey Mowgli had ever seen before, and the rest of the creatures seemed to clear a path for them.

'Man cub!' said the giant monkey, bounding over to Mowgli and stopping just a few inches from his face. 'We have wanted you to join us for so long!'

'Take me back!' demanded

Mowgli. 'I want to go back to Bagheera and Baloo!'

The monkey threw back his head and laughed, sending the rest of the monkeys into fits of laughter too. 'That old bear and stuffy, boring panther?' he asked. 'You'd rather be with *them* than with us?'

'Yes I would! They've never kidnapped me!' said Mowgli.

The large monkey placed a hand on his chest. His eyes grew wide in pretend horror. 'My dear man cub!' he said. 'We didn't *kidnap* you. We just extended a polite invitation for you to join us in our humble home!'

Mowgli folded his arms and scowled.

'Let me introduce myself. My name is Bandar,' said the giant monkey. 'As you can see, we

live in the most advanced, most civilised part of the jungle. We're not just a pack of wild animals running through the trees. We are as good as humans. Well, almost. And that is why we *gently* persuaded you to come here today.'

'Why do you need *me*?' said Mowgli. 'I don't know anything about being a human. I'm part of the wolf pack.'

Bandar circled Mowgli,

prodding his tummy and lifting his arms and legs in turn. 'Man cub, you are *not* a wolf,' he said. 'Whether you like it or not, you are human. And you are going to stay with us until you teach us everything you know.

We want to know how to build houses like these ancient ruins once were. We want to know how to make clothes. But most of all, we want to know how to make the red flower. Tell us how to make fire!'

Mowgli jumped up. 'But I don't know any of those things!' he cried.

Bandar stepped closer to Mowgli. His hot breath on Mowgli's face. 'Then you had better learn, quickly.'

Meanwhile, Bagheera and Baloo reached the fast-flowing river. They knew the ruins were close, but Bagheera suddenly stopped. 'What are you doing?' asked Baloo. 'We've got to keep moving!'

'We need Kaa,' said Bagheera calmly. 'There are hundreds of monkeys at the ancient ruins doing whatever Bandar asks of them. Kaa is the only creature in the jungle that Bandar is afraid of.'

Baloo stepped back. 'I'm not going

anywhere near that slithering snake,' he said. 'One look in her eyes and you're done for!'

'That may be true but Kaa's also greedy,' replied Bagheera, sniffing the air for any trace of scent of the giant python. 'If we promise her a whole camp of monkeys in return for her help in rescuing Mowgli, she won't be interested in eating us.'

Kaa slithered around the trunk of the hollowed-out tree she called her home.

She smiled, knowingly, at Baloo and Bagheera. 'You mussst *really* need help if you have come to me,' she hissed. 'What makesss you think I will help you? The man cub meansss nothing to me.' Kaa thought for a moment before widening her jaws in a wicked grin. 'Asside from perhapsss a tasssty sssnack!'

Baloo cleared his throat. 'Kaa, you know Bandar is afraid of you,' he began. 'All you have to do is show up at the ancient ruins and you can have your pick of a hundred monkeys. All we ask is that you let Baloo and I take Mowgli to safety.'

Kaa's tongue flicked in and out of her mouth as she considered Bagheera's request.

She looked at Baloo and tried not to laugh as the bear avoided her mesmerising gaze. 'I sssuppose I could do you thisss favour,' she said, lazily at last. 'But make no missstake. This isss a one-time offer.

Do not think that becaussse of thisss we are friendsss.'

'Ha! Don't you worry about that!' joked Baloo, then quickly fell silent again.

'Thank you, Kaa,' said Bagheera. He turned to lead the snake towards the ruins.

Baloo carefully climbed on a fallen pillar and stretched his neck as high as he could to see over the walls of the ancient ruins. 'Can you see him?' whispered Bagheera.

'He's in there all right,' said Baloo. 'Bandar's got his arm around him, locked tight!'

'Then what are we waiting out here for?' asked Kaa, slithering her huge body along the walls. 'You aren't afraid of a sssilly bunch of sssimians, are you?'

Baloo backed away from Kaa to let her glide past, over the wall and into the ruins. When they heard the terrified cries of the monkeys, Baloo and Bagheera followed her in.

simians

The name of the species given to monkeys and apes.

The monkeys leapt this way and that, trying to get as far away from Kaa and her hypnotic eyes as they could.

The giant python cleared a path for Baloo and Bagheera to reach Mowgli. She then slithered off to select her next meal from the scattering monkeys. Bandar stood still, not taking his arm from around the boy.

'Let him go, Bandar, and there won't be any more trouble,' said Bagheera.

'Oh, I can't do that,' replied Bandar, smiling a wide, toothy grin.

'Not when he's having such a good time here!'

'No, I'm not!' cried Mowgli.

'You let him go or we'll leave Kaa here to eat the lot of you!' said Baloo.

Bandar looked around at his band of frightened monkeys, then back at Mowgli, trying to decide.

With a sigh and a scowl, he released his grip. Mowgli ran into the safe, warm arms of Baloo. 'Call off your snake!' said Bandar. 'But don't think you've won, man cub. Shere Khan is back, and he has vowed not to rest until you are out of the jungle. Or dead.'

Both Baloo and Bagheera had already heard this news through the mutterings of the jungle. Mowgli would have to make a tough choice: to stay and fight Shere Khan or flee the jungle, forever.

Chapter Six

A few days later, Mowgli was playing with Grey outside the wolf den. They tumbled, fought and laughed, watched over by Mother Wolf. Mowgli tried to put all thought of Shere Khan out of his mind as he lazed in the sun and lapped water from the watering hole, but the tiger kept creeping into his head.

'Mother Wolf, have you heard?' Father Wolf ran into the den, his eyes wild. 'It's Akela. We were out on a hunt and he … he missed his prey!'

Mowgli and Grey looked at each other in shock. Not only was it unheard of that Akela would fail to succeed while out hunting, but they both knew what would happen next. According to the law of the wolf pack, if the alpha wolf misses their prey, they are no longer the leader. A new wolf would be chosen.

'Poor Akela!' said Mother

Wolf, getting to her feet. 'What happens now?'

'The council will be called to find a new leader,' replied Father Wolf.

'You can be the leader, Dad!' said Grey, bouncing playfully onto his father's back.

Father Wolf smiled sadly at his cub, then looked up at Mowgli with concern in his eyes. 'I am too old, now,' he said. 'The pack will need someone younger and stronger and–' he paused. 'I do not know what this will mean for you, Mowgli.'

Mother Wolf padded next to Mowgli. 'What do you mean?' she asked.

'Mowgli only had the protection of the pack because of Akela's decision,' explained Father Wolf. 'The pack obeyed him because he was the leader, but not all the wolves were happy about going against Shere Khan. We must be prepared, my boy. If the new leader sides with the tiger, I don't know what we are going to do.'

That night, while Mother Wolf

obey

To follow instructions or orders.

settled her cubs into the den, Father Wolf made his way to Council Rock. Bagheera, having heard of Akela's fall from leadership, took his spot on a nearby tree branch to listen in. He nodded a silent greeting as Father Wolf sat down at the back of the pack.

As the moon shone, an elderly wolf with silver and grey fur took his place on the high rock where Akela once stood. 'My brothers, we are here to choose a new leader,' said the old wolf. 'Who among you has the strength to lead and guide our pack?'

Silence fell over the wolves. Heads turned and paws scratched the ground, but no one came forwards. 'What is happening?' asked Bagheera, smoothly jumping down from his branch to sit with Father Wolf.

'No one wants to take Akela's place,' said Father Wolf.

'Surely that's a good thing, for Mowgli at least?' asked Bagheera.

Father Wolf shook his head. 'A pack without a leader gets frightened. As soon as Shere Khan knows we are leaderless, Mowgli will be in more danger than ever.'

Chapter Seven

Mowgli had not been out of the wolf den for three days and three nights. Each evening, Father Wolf would sit at the entrance to their cave, on the same spot they first found Mowgli, and watch for any sign of Shere Khan. The pack could still not decide on a wolf to become the leader, and the wolves were in confusion.

'Can't I just go and see Baloo?' whined Mowgli as he watched his brothers leave the den for a day of play. 'He'd keep me safe, I know it!'

Mother Wolf placed a paw on Mowgli's hand.

'I'm sorry, son,' she said gently. 'Until the pack has a new leader it isn't safe.'

'Quiet!' barked Father Wolf, standing at the mouth of the cave, his nose sniffing the air. 'Someone is coming.'

Mother Wolf stood protectively in front of Mowgli as two young wolves emerged from the trees.

'What do you want?' asked Father Wolf, who lowered his body and bared his teeth just a little to give the visitors a warning.

'There is no need to be like that,' said one of the wolves.

'All we want is the man cub,' said the other. 'Shere Khan knows the pack is without a leader and he could strike us at any time.'

'If we hand over the man cub,' added the first wolf, 'Shere Khan will leave us alone. It is for the good of the pack.'

Mother Wolf joined Father Wolf

at the front of the cave and gave a low growl of warning. 'You leave my cub alone,' she said. 'He is part of the pack, and he is protected!'

The young wolves shook their manes. 'Not anymore,' said the second wolf. 'You have until sunset to bring the man cub to Council Rock, or we will be back to take him.'

Mowgli hugged his knees as he watched the two wolves disappear back into the jungle. He had never been frightened of any wolf before in his life. Their teeth and claws were as familiar to him as his own hands and feet.

For the first time, Mowgli was aware of how fragile he was compared to these powerful creatures.

'Fetch Baloo and Bagheera,' Mother Wolf told Father Wolf. 'If the pack won't protect Mowgli, we'll need as much help as we can find.'

As the sun cast shadows on the jungle floor, Mowgli watched Mother and Father Wolf as they talked with Baloo and Bagheera. From within the cave, it was hard to hear what they were saying. Mowgli grabbed a small rock from the floor and carried on drawing on the cave walls. He wanted to finish his picture of Shere Khan running far away from the jungle, with Mowgli standing tall on Council Rock.

'Little man, come out here!' called Baloo.

Mowgli dropped his rock and slowly walked out into the sunshine. The light hurt his eyes after so many days in the den.

'Son, we have decided to take you to the man village,' said Mother Wolf, softly.

Mowgli stepped back in shock. He looked between the faces of his friends and his wolf parents. At that moment, Grey came out of the trees, hot from playing with his brothers and sisters.

'You can't make me!' cried Mowgli. 'I won't go!'

'Go where?' asked Grey, padding

over to sit next to Mowgli.

'They are forcing me to leave the jungle, to go back to the man village!' shouted Mowgli.

'It is the only way to keep you safe, my son,' said Father Wolf. 'The man village is surrounded by the red flower. It is the only thing that Shere Khan is afraid of.'

Grey placed a paw on Mowgli's shoulder. 'But Mowgli has the protection of the pack!' he said. 'You can't make him leave, he's my brother!'

Mother Wolf nuzzled Grey as a

single tear ran down her nose.

'I don't want you to leave, Mowgli,' she said. 'But I would rather you left and lived, than stayed in the jungle and died.'

Bagheera slowly stepped forwards. 'Mowgli, it has been decided that Baloo and I will take you to the man village,' he said. 'But you must come now. It is almost sunset and Shere Khan will not wait.'

'Come on, kid,' said Baloo, patting his back. 'Jump on.'

Mowgli stared in disbelief. Tears stung the back of his eyes. He did not want to leave his family or the only home he had ever known, but he knew he had no choice. He threw his arms around his mother's mane, pressed his forehead to his father's, then clambered onto Baloo's strong back.

As they walked away, he tried to block out the sound of Grey's whimpering.

The path to the man village was through a part of the jungle Mowgli had never been to before. Even though it was unfamiliar to him, Mowgli made sure to remember each tree, each twist and turn and *every* rock. He wanted to be sure he could find his way back to the wolf den, and to Council Rock, if he needed to.

As the last wisps of sunlight danced across the sky, the thick jungle opened up to reveal a fast-flowing river.

Just beyond were the burning torches that surrounded the man village.

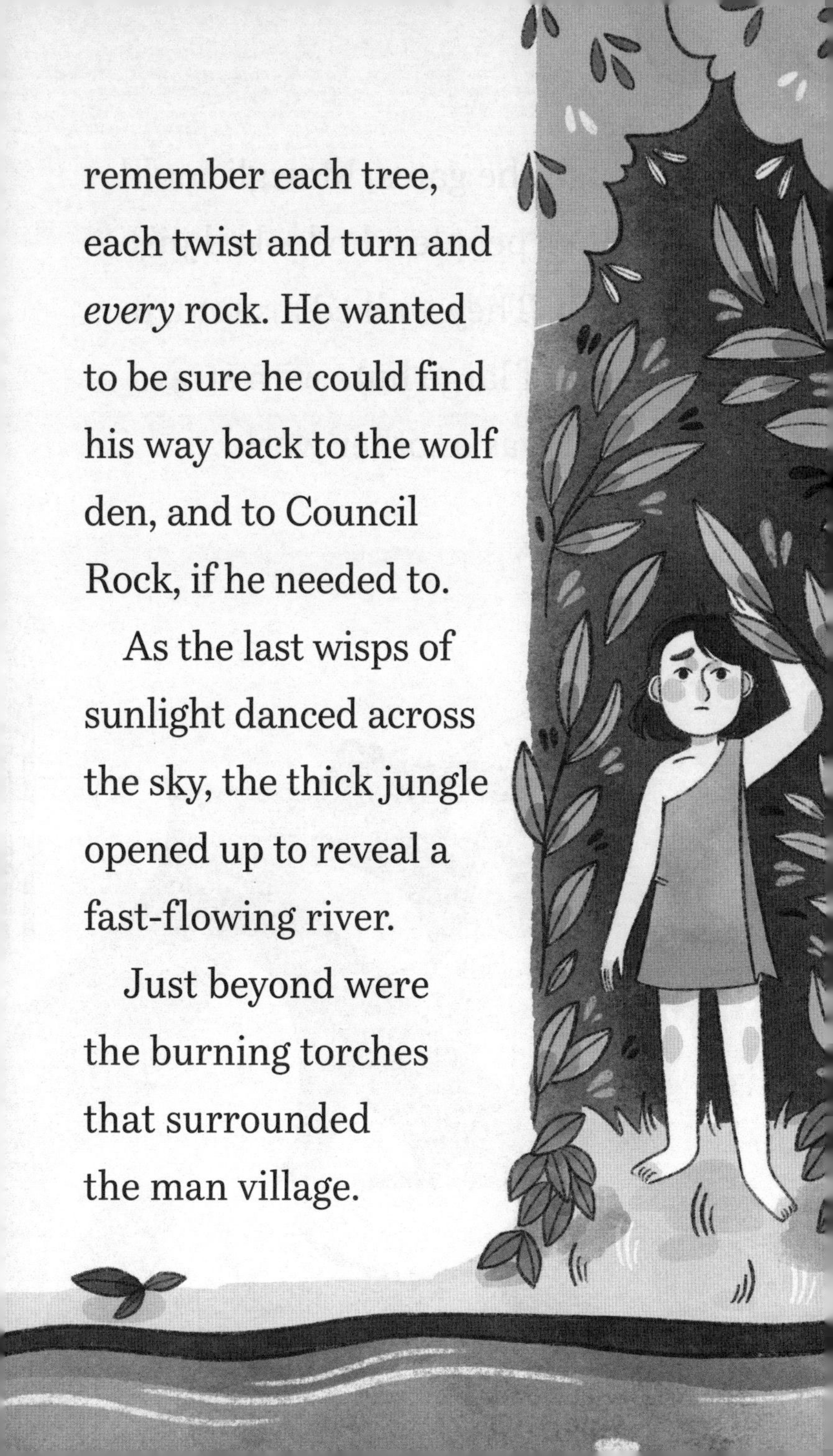

Through the gates, Mowgli could see other people who looked just like him. They walked around, in and out of large huts with straw roofs. It was another world.

‘The red flower is what will protect you,’ said Bagheera, helping Mowgli down off Baloo’s back. ‘Shere Khan is terrified of it.’

‘As long as you keep on that side of the fence, little man, you’ll be safe,’ said Baloo.

With one last glance at his friends, Mowgli walked away. He just hoped it wouldn’t be forever.

Chapter Eight

‘The red flower,’ repeated Mowgli. Its flames licked the air, giving off a thin stream of smoke as he entered the man village.

‘Who are you?’ asked a tall man. He was holding a torch, and Mowgli couldn't help but stare at him. It was fascinating to see a grown human for the first time.

He walked on two legs like Mowgli and had thick hair sprouting from his chin. The man's words made no sense in Mowgli's head. He had not heard a human talk since he was a baby.

'Which village are you from?' the man tried again. 'How have you got here?'

Mowgli continued to stare at the man, blankly, until a woman came up behind him and his eyes grew wide. This human was different to himself and the man, too. 'Who is this?' she asked, smiling kindly at Mowgli.

'I don't know, Messua, the boy won't tell me,' replied the man. 'Looks like he's just wandered straight out of the jungle!'

Messua leant down so that she was face to face with Mowgli. 'Will you come with me?' she asked, placing a warm hand on Mowgli's shoulder.

Mowgli glanced back to the gate of the man village. He wondered if Baloo and Bagheera were watching him still. With a small sigh, he turned to follow the woman.

Messua lived in a large mud-built house with rooms for eating, sleeping and washing. To Mowgli, it seemed like a gigantic cave, but one where he did not have to stoop or crouch.

He sat on the floor until Messua showed him the table and chairs.

That night, Messua took Mowgli to the centre of the man village, where a crowd had gathered. Mowgli noticed that there were smaller humans, just like him, and even smaller ones, too.

It reminded Mowgli of Council Rock, but instead of Akela at the head of the pack, there was a man with grey hair and long robes.

'Messua, bring the child to me!' demanded the man.

Messua held Mowgli's hand as she led him forward. 'Chief, I believe this boy has been living wild,' she said. 'He doesn't understand our language and he doesn't know how simple things like a chair, or a bed, or even a bowl work. With the permission of the village, I would like to take him in.'

Mowgli looked up at the chief. He knew that this man was important. Perhaps as important as Akela had once been to the pack. He bowed his head a little, and when he glanced back up, he could see the chief was smiling.

'Very well,' said the chief at last. 'We shall give the boy a home here.'

Chapter Nine

Messua taught Mowgli the laws of the man village. Although he missed Mother Wolf and his family in the jungle, he felt a connection with Messua that he had never experienced before.

He soon picked up the language the humans used. He learnt how to wash in the river and marvelled at the way his hair felt when Messua scrubbed and cut it.

The clothes she made him wear

were scratchy at first, and he longed to take them off, but he could see every other child in the village had the same clothes on, so he did as he was told.

Mowgli could not get used to his bed. He struggled to sleep on something so soft. One night, when Messua was asleep, he snuck out of the house to find something more suitable.

He reached the edge of the man village. Mowgli stared out across the thick, dark trees of the jungle, imagining what Mother and Father Wolf were doing.

'Mowgli!' whispered a hushed voice.

'Grey? Is that you?' asked Mowgli.

Grey was crouched in the shadow of the man village. 'Mowgli! I've missed you so much!' he cried.

Mowgli hugged his brother. 'Grey! What are you doing here? It's not safe.'

'I came to see you,' replied Grey. 'Shere Khan is still hunting you. He's angry that you managed to leave without his knowledge.'

Mowgli sighed. 'Does he know where I am?' he asked.

'Not yet, but it's only a matter of time,' replied Grey. 'He has threatened the whole jungle to tell him where you are.'

Mowgli glanced back to the man village. 'I should get back,' he said. 'If Messua wakes and finds me gone she will be worried.'

Grey stepped back. 'Who is Messua?' he asked.

Mowgli stroked his brother's mane. 'Messua is looking after me,' he said reassuringly. 'Tell Mother that I am being cared for. Messua reminds me of her but she will never replace Mother Wolf in my heart. You will always be my family.'

As the weeks passed, Mowgli began to feel that he was being accepted into the man village. He was given a job helping to look after the herds of buffalo that the villagers kept.

Everyone was amazed at how well Mowgli handled the animals but, of course, they didn't realise that he was able talk to them using the Master Words he had learnt from Bagheera and Baloo. He simply explained to the buffalo where they needed to go and why.

Some of the farmers were confused by and even jealous of

his skill, but Mowgli ignored their strange looks.

Grey continued to visit Mowgli as often as he could. They agreed that Grey would come to the village each full moon, and when he did, he brought news of home.

The wolf pack still couldn't decide on a leader, so there were many arguments among the group. Hunts that used to be done as a pack were now happening in small groups and no one had enough to eat.

One full moon, Mowgli waited for Grey to visit, but that night, he didn't come. It was the first time he had not shown up.

Mowgli's throat tightened with fear.

The following night, Mowgli snuck out of Messua's house and waited. Again, Grey didn't show up.

On the third night after the full moon, at last Grey came. 'I am sorry, Mowgli,' he said, out of breath from running. 'I could not get away. The wolf pack have been meeting most nights, they are arguing over what to do about Shere Khan.'

'What do you mean?' asked Mowgli, urgently.

'Shere Khan says he's had enough of waiting. He's planning on attacking the pack unless they help him to capture you.'

Mowgli felt a trembling of anger deep in his chest. Shere Khan had forced him out of his home and still it wasn't enough. Now, he was causing division in the pack. 'What can I do to help?' asked Mowgli.

Grey shook his mane. 'There is nothing that can be done,' he said, sadly. 'But I had to come and see you. I may not be able to get away until things have calmed down for us. Stay safe, brother.'

Mowgli touched his forehead to Grey's. 'And you, brother.'

Chapter Ten

Mowgli woke to the sound of angry voices. A group of men had turned up at Messua's house, demanding to speak to her about 'the boy'.

'We saw him, Messua,' shouted one of the men. 'As plain as I am standing here talking to you, the boy was talking to a wolf!'

'That's nonsense!' said Messua. 'We don't know much about the life he had before he came to the village but to say he can talk to animals is just …'

'Madness? Witchcraft? *Sorcery*?' replied one of the men. At that moment, Mowgli appeared behind Messua. 'Oh, here he is. The wolf boy. We always wondered how you had such a good touch with the buffalo and now we know!'

Mowgli looked up at Messua with wide eyes, not daring to speak.

'Excuse me, but we have not even had our breakfast yet,' said

sorcery
The practice of magic.

Messua, standing protectively in front of Mowgli in a way that reminded him very much of Mother Wolf. 'And I would thank you to leave us in peace.'

But even though the men walked away, they did not leave Mowgli in peace. Each time he stepped outside Messua's house, they were there. Watching him. Waiting for him to do something that would prove their claims.

News of Mowgli's talk with Grey spread across the village. Children would whisper as he made his way to the buffalo field, and soon the farmers stopped asking him to help them.

Mowgli was lonely. He had always felt different in the jungle, and he knew he was not like the other animals, but he was never made to feel isolated. He was never an outsider.

The only person to comfort him was Messua. She knew Mowgli better than anyone in the village. She also knew in her heart this wasn't where Mowgli belonged.

That night, he could not sleep. Although it was not a full moon,

isolated

To feel separated and alone.

he made his way through the darkness of the village to the spot where he usually met Grey. He looked out at the thick, dark jungle, hoping for a sign to tell him what he should do. And then it came.

Out of the dark, a pair of yellow, shining eyes appeared. Mowgli froze. His heart beat faster as he recognised Shere Khan.

The tiger slowly prowled through the trees – his eyes flickered to the red flower that surrounded the village and Mowgli knew he would not come any closer. Shere Khan stared at Mowgli, daring him to move. The boy stood, willing his legs not to tremble. He would not show the tiger that he was afraid of him.

After a moment, Shere Khan gave a small, wicked smile. He then turned and padded casually back to the jungle. And Mowgli knew what he had to do.

The following day, Mowgli told Messua he would be at work in the fields. Instead, he spent his time making a torch, just like the ones he had seen the older men use at nighttime to walk around the village.

He gathered dried reeds from the riverside and a branch to use as a handle. He found some old rope and tied it all together. He knew it would have to be large and burn fiercely for his plan to work.

That evening, he sat at Messua's table and ate dinner with her. He knew this might be the last time he would see her, and it hurt him that she didn't know it. But he didn't want to cause her any more pain than he had to. Mowgli had made a decision. He was going to go back to the jungle to face Shere Khan himself.

It was the only way to restore peace in the wolf pack and to stop Shere Khan from terrorising the family he loved. There was only one thing Mowgli could use to fight the tiger. The one thing Shere Khan feared. The red flower.

As soon as Messua was fast asleep, he took the torch out from under his bed and quietly left the house.

The flames of the fire furiously danced as Mowgli lit the torch. Then, as fast as he could, he ran into the jungle, back along the path he had memorised on the way to the man village.

Mowgli's legs burned with exhaustion as he reached Council Rock. There, a huge crowd of wolves and other animals sat. He sprinted through them, holding his torch above him.

'I'm not afraid!' Mowgli shouted. 'I will not hide any longer!'

The wolves gazed in shock at the returned

man cub and it was only then that Mowgli glanced up to the highest point of the rock and saw who was standing there. Shere Khan.

'Well, well,' drawled Shere Khan. 'You have finally returned to us. We *have* missed you.'

'Mowgli! What are you doing!' cried Father Wolf, running over to stand by his son.

Shere Khan leapt from the rock. The pack of wolves scattered to the edges of the clearing, leaving Mowgli and Father Wolf alone. 'You see, the pack won't protect you,' chuckled Shere Khan.

The flickering of the red flower reflecting in his eyes.

'The pack might not,' said Father Wolf. 'But I will.'

'As will I!' said Akela, bounding out from the crowd to join Father Wolf. It was the first time anyone had seen him since the failed hunt many months ago.

'How very touching,' said Shere Khan. 'It's a shame that an old wolf, a fallen leader and a scrawny man cub are no match for me.'

Mowgli leapt forward, swinging his torch in front of the giant tiger. Shere Khan jumped back, growling and hissing. Mowgli could sense Shere Khan's fear. Mowgli moved closer, waving the torch wildly so that embers flew off in each direction. 'You will keep the red flower away from me if you know what is good for you,' said Shere Khan, the smallest hint of a tremble in his voice.

'Or what?' demanded a voice that filled Mowgli with joy.

embers

Pieces of glowing wood or coal that burn without a flame.

Baloo had come to stand with him and behind was Bagheera, poised and ready to attack.

Chapter Eleven

Shere Khan bared his teeth as Father Wolf and Akela surrounded him. They snapped at his paws, making Shere Khan unsteady on his feet. Baloo took Mowgli on his back to raise him above the tiger as Bagheera swiped with his claws.

As Baloo bounded closer, Mowgli swung the torch and set fire to the tiger's tail.

'What have you done?' roared Shere Khan, dancing this way and that, desperate to get away from the flame.

Akela and Father Wolf pounced on Shere Khan, but the tiger was still strong enough to throw them off.

‘We’ll take it from here, little man,’ said Baloo, setting Mowgli on the ground before joining Bagheera and the wolves in the fight. The fire on Shere Khan’s tail was growing stronger.

Mowgli took his chance. He ran to the highest point on the rock. ‘Leave the jungle!’ cried Mowgli. ‘Leave now and never come back!’

Terror rose in Shere Khan's face as he looked from the wolves to Baloo to Bagheera. The rest of the pack saw that the tiger was losing his power, and they lined up in support behind the fighting friends.

Shere Khan turned and raced away into the jungle, the light from his tail becoming smaller and smaller as he fled into the night.

Mowgli dropped the torch onto the hard ground of Council Rock and sat down, exhausted, as the fire finally dwindled. Akela nuzzled into his side and Mowgli flopped an arm around his mane.

The animals who had hidden in fear slowly began to reappear from the jungle, filling Council Rock and staring at the man cub who had defeated the great Shere Khan. Baloo and Bagheera watched in wonder as each wolf sat obediently in front of Mowgli and Akela.

Father Wolf padded next to Mowgli and Akela. 'My friends, we have been leaderless for too long,' he said, looking down at the pack. 'After this night, it is clear who our leaders should be. Akela, will you be our alpha once again, with Mowgli by your side?'

The wolves howled together in agreement as Akela and Mowgli gazed at each other. 'You mean, I can stay in the jungle?' asked Mowgli.

'All this time we thought we were the ones offering you protection,' replied Father Wolf with a smile. 'When really you are the one who will protect us. This is where you belong.' Father Wolf nuzzled Mowgli and they hugged knowing that they would never be parted again.

Rudyard Kipling

Rudyard Kipling was born in Mumbai, India in 1865. At the age of six, Kipling was taken to England by his parents and left at a foster home before being placed into boarding school. Years later he returned to India. His popularity as a writer grew as he wrote poetry and fiction in his free time. His famous works, such as *The Jungle Book*, led him to receive the Nobel Prize for Literature in 1907.